Explore the World of
Marvelous Machines

Text by Brian Williams
Illustrated by Sebastian Quigley

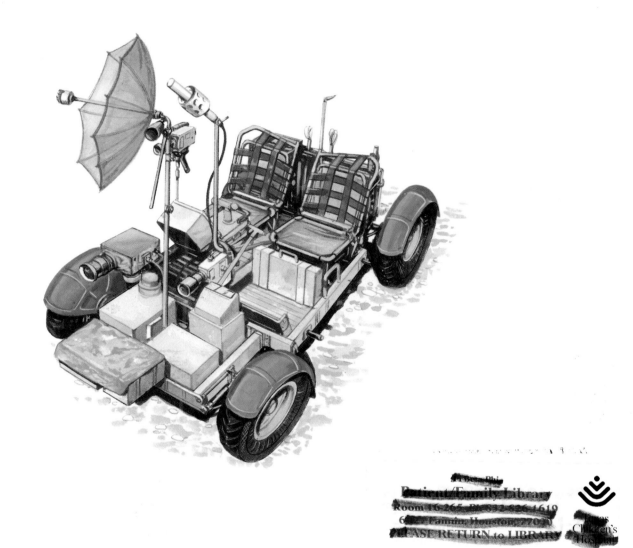

A GOLDEN BOOK • NEW YORK
Western Publishing Company, Inc., Racine, Wisconsin 53404

Contents

How big is a supertanker?
A modern tanker is as high as a twenty-story building and longer than three football fields. The world's largest ships are supertankers.

Why are racing cars streamlined?

Racing cars are low and sleek. They have a smooth, "streamlined" shape for two reasons: First, a smooth shape cuts easily through the air. Any air resistance can slow a car down, so its streamlined shape helps the racing car to go faster. Second, as the air rushes over the racing car's low, flat body, it forces the car downwards. A racing car, therefore, can travel more quickly around turns than a car which is not streamlined.

More about automobile racing

Automobile racing began in 1895, when twenty-two cars raced between Paris and Bordeaux, in France. The first Grand Prix race was run in 1906 at Le Mans, in France. The drivers of the early racing cars sat upright behind big steering wheels. Today's drivers lie almost flat, and the steering wheel is small.

The driver races at speeds of more than 200 miles per hour. If a racing car crashes, the greatest danger is fire. Racing drivers wear overalls made of up to five layers of flameproof material. The driver's helmet has a visor that is also flameproof. Underneath, the driver wears a Balaclava face mask. Flameproof gloves and lightweight boots complete the driver's clothing.

Why do trucks have gears?

A truck driver uses gears to control the power output from the truck's engine. The engine drives a shaft that is connected to the truck's wheels through a transmission. Inside the transmission is an arrangement of different sized wheels with notches, or teeth, around their edges. The teeth on one wheel fit into the notches on the next wheel. Each wheel has a different number of teeth, and so turns at a different speed. Gears, therefore, can make the truck's wheels turn faster or slower. Low gears are used for greater power when moving heavy loads or going uphill, and on a flat road, the higher gears are used to go faster.

What is motocross?

Motocross is an exciting form of motorcycle racing. Another name for motocross is scrambling. Motocross began in Europe but is now popular all over the world. The riders race their bikes over rugged cross-country courses that wind up and down hills, into streams, and through thick mud or sand. There are championships for motorcycles with engines of 125, 250, and 500 cc (cubic centimeters). The motorcycles are stripped of all nonessential fittings and have special rough-riding tires. When the riders race over a bank or hilltop, the motorcycles sometimes leave the ground. It takes great skill to land safely and roar on over the bumpy ground at top speed.

More about motorcycles

A sidecar turns a two-wheeled bike into a three-wheeler. In a sidecar race, the sidecar passenger lies flat. On turns the passenger either leans across the bike or swings out the other way, almost touching the track, as the bike and sidecar hurtle around the curves at high speed.

As a motorcycle rider takes a turn, centrifugal force tends to push the bike outward. To counter this push, the rider leans into the turn. On a sharp curve, a race rider often leans so far to one side that his leg brushes the ground as the machine speeds around the track.

Racing tires are different from road tires. They are broader at the bottom, to give extra grip on the road as the bike races round a curve.

Where do dragsters race?

Dragsters are special racing cars. They are designed to go very fast over a short distance. The cars race along a straight track called a strip, which is only one quarter of a mile long. Two cars take part in each race, which begins from a standing start. As soon as the drivers see the green light for "go," they accelerate as fast as they can. The race is over in a few seconds. Some dragsters are converted road cars with "souped-up" engines. Others with weird-looking fiberglass bodies are known as funny cars. Rail dragsters have pencil-slim bodies, with big wheels at the back.

More about drag racing

The United States is the home of professional drag racing. The fastest time by a piston-engined drag racer is 4.99 seconds. The funny car shown above and rail dragsters have piston engines burning an alcohol-based fuel instead of gasoline. They are called Eliminator cars.

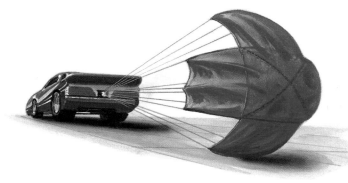

The fastest drag racers cross the finish line at over 155 miles per hour. A funny car holds the record time for a dragster — just over 3.5 seconds from start to finish. As these cars race at such high speeds braking parachutes are needed to bring them safely to a stop.

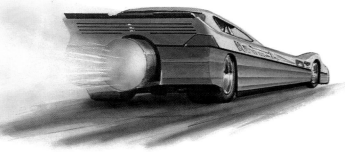

A dragster must make a quick getaway. At the start line, each driver warms up his tires by racing the engine so they spin furiously. The hotter the tires, the better they grip the track. Some dragsters have rocket or jet engines. These super-dragsters can accelerate to 600 miles per hour.

How do underground trains work?

Underground trains, or subways, carry passengers beneath busy cities. The trains run through tunnels dug beneath the city streets. The first underground railway was opened in London in 1863. The system used steam trains, which filled the tunnels with smoke. Electric trains were introduced in the 1890s, and today all underground railways use electric trains. The trains run at between 10 and 50 miles per hour. They have drivers, but there are also computerized signal systems for safety. Moscow has the most impressive underground stations, with marble walls and golden decorations.

More about transport on land

What was the first steam vehicle?

A Frenchman named Nicolas Cugnot built a steam-driven gun carriage in 1763 *(below, right)*. It was very slow, and people were afraid of it. It had a carriage with three wheels and a large boiler which stuck out in front. The engine could only run for ten or twelve minutes and reached a speed of up to 6 miles per hour. A second version of the vehicle was so uncontrollable, it ran into and demolished a wall. The first successful steam road vehicle was Richard Trevithick's steam coach of 1801 *(below, left)*. Trevithick later drove another steam coach from Cornwall to London, England.

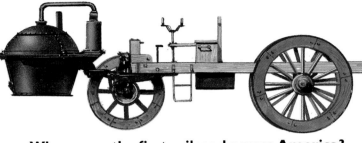

Where was the first railroad across America?

On May 10, 1869, the tracks of the Union Pacific and Central Pacific railroads were joined at Promontory, Utah. For the first time America could be crossed by train *(below)*. The building of the railroad began in 1863, with the Union Pacific laying track from the east, and the Central Pacific starting from the west.

Which was the fastest steam train?

In July 1938 the British locomotive *Mallard* set a world speed record for steam. It reached a speed of almost 126 miles per hour, hauling a train of seven cars which weighed a total of 240 tons. *Mallard* was operated by the London and North Eastern Railway.

Where was the first electric train seen?

The first electric train was demonstrated in Germany in 1879 *(above)*. The first mainline electric railway was operated by the Baltimore and Ohio Railroad in 1895. The world's first diesel locomotive was built in Germany in 1912 *(right)*. Diesel trains came into service in the 1920s.

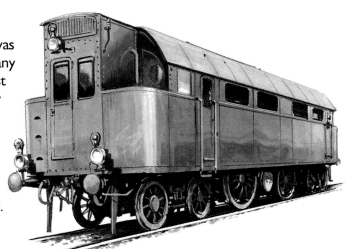

What was a "Tin Lizzie?"

"Tin Lizzie" was the nickname of the Ford Model T, built from 1908 to 1927. It was the first mass-production car.

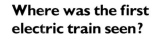

What is the most popular car?

The best-selling car ever is the Volkswagen "Beetle." This German model was first built in 1938 and continued in production into the 1980s. More than 21 million "Beetles" have been made in factories in Germany and in other countries.

Where was the motorbike invented?

The first motorized bicycle *(above)* was built in Germany in 1885 by Gottlieb Daimler.

How fast can a car travel?

Jet and rocket cars can travel much faster than a conventional car. The world's land speed record is held by the jet-engined car *Thrust 2*. In 1983 it reached a speed of 650 miles per hour across the Black Rock Desert in Nevada.

INITIAL SERVICES   turbo FOR MEN   Castrol   THRUST 2   PLESSEY   LOCTITE LOCTITE   Trust Securities   CHAMPION   TRIMITE

How fast can trains travel?

The fastest train on any national railroad system is the French TGV, or high-speed train. This bullet-shaped, streamlined electric train has traveled at 305 miles per hour, which is about half as fast as an ordinary passenger jet plane. Normally the TGV runs at about 168 miles per hour. High-speed trains travel on special high-speed track, with no sharp turns or gradients (hills). On ordinary track, electric locomotives can haul a passenger train at speeds of around 137 miles per hour.

More about trains

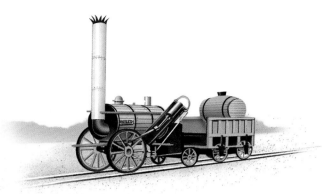

George Stephenson, a British engineer, built the *Rocket,* a steam locomotive which, in 1829, outstripped all rivals in a contest to find the fastest railway engine. The *Rocket* reached a speed of 36 miles per hour astonishing the spectators. The *Rocket* was used to pull passenger trains on the Liverpool and Manchester Railway.

Some electric trains pick up an electric current from overhead wires through a pantograph. The pantograph is fixed to the top of the locomotive and slides along the wires. Other electric trains (such as subways) pick up electric power from a third rail alongside the track.

Maglev (magnetic levitation) trains are very fast experimental trains. They ride just above a metal track, and are driven by powerful magnets. The Japanese maglev system in Tokyo whisks passengers to the city's airport.

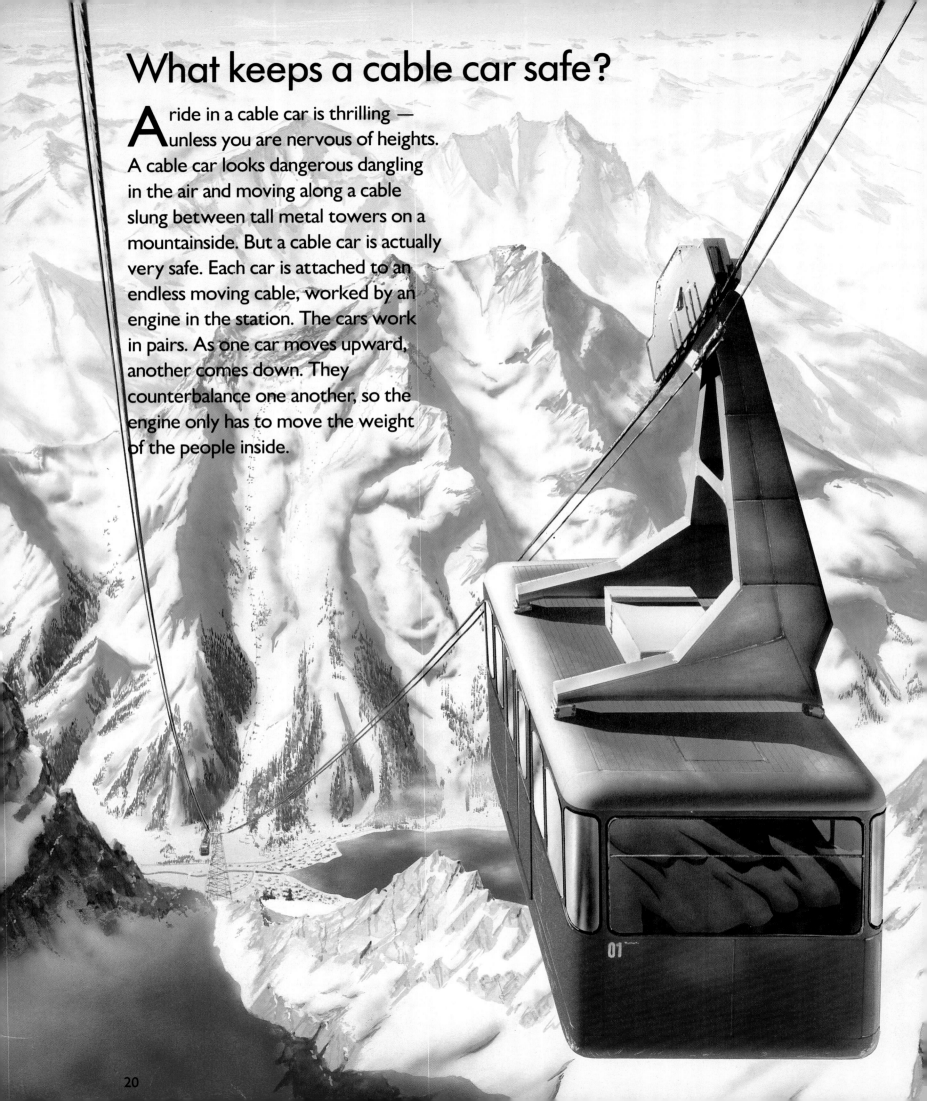

What keeps a cable car safe?

A ride in a cable car is thrilling — unless you are nervous of heights. A cable car looks dangerous dangling in the air and moving along a cable slung between tall metal towers on a mountainside. But a cable car is actually very safe. Each car is attached to an endless moving cable, worked by an engine in the station. The cars work in pairs. As one car moves upward, another comes down. They counterbalance one another, so the engine only has to move the weight of the people inside.

More about mountainside transport

A funicular railway works on the counterweight principle. Two cars are attached to either end of a cable running over pulleys. As one car goes up, the other goes down. Some funiculars have engines driving the pulley. Others rely entirely on gravity: The cars have water tanks that are filled to go down, emptied to go up.

Cog railways run up mountain slopes that are too steep for ordinary locomotives, whose wheels would slip on the rails. The cog railway locomotive has a toothed driving wheel that runs along a notched, or racked, rail on the track. The teeth prevent the train from slipping backward.

Cable elevators were built to carry tourists up to vantage points on top of very steep clifftops and mountains. The old lattice girder elevator to Burgenstock, Switzerland, provides visitors with splendid views across Lake Lucerne.

How can a hovercraft cross land and water?

A hovercraft travels on a cushion of air. This explains its other name of air-cushion vehicle, or ACV for short. The air is blown down underneath the craft by fans, and kept in place by a flexible skirt. The hovercraft's main engines drive propellers which can be turned to propel the craft forward, backward or sideways. Because they do not actually touch the surface, hovercraft can travel across land or water.

More about hovercraft

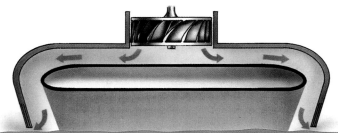

The flexible skirt of a hovercraft is made from a tough rubberlike material. The skirt keeps the cushion of air in place to support the craft. It also allows the hovercraft to ride over obstacles such as tree trunks or sandbanks without losing air from the cushion and sinking to earth. Some ACVs have rigid sidewalls to do the same job.

A conventional speedboat or hydroplane rises partly out of the water at high speed. The less the boat touches the surface, the less friction (rubbing) there is between the hull and the water. The record speed by a hydroplane is 317.3 miles per hour.

A hydrofoil is a craft with underwater "wings," or foils beneath the hull. The foils are submerged when the craft is at rest. When the hydrofoil accelerates, the foils are lifted by the force of water passing over them. They raise the hull clear of the water, and the hydrofoil skims over the surface at speeds of up to 62 miles per hour. The angle of the foils can be altered to give different amounts of "lift."

What is the fastest plane?

The holder of the world speed record for a jet plane is the U.S. Air Force's SR-71A Blackbird spy-plane shown here. In 1976 this top-secret jet set a speed record of 2,192 miles per hour. The Blackbird was retired from Air Force duties in 1989.

Even the Blackbird would have been left behind by the X-15 rocket plane which reached a speed of 4,531 miles per hour. Aircraft speeds are often given in Mach numbers. Mach 1 is the speed of sound, which is 740 miles per hour at sea level. The fastest jets are capable of Mach 2.3.

24

More flying feats

The Boeing B-52 bomber first flew in 1952, but still serves with the U.S. Air Force. It has an enormous wingspan, measuring 185 feet from wingtip to wingtip. The eight jet engines that power this mighty machine are carried under the wings.

Aerobatic displays by crack teams such as the U.S. Airforce Thunderbirds and the British R.A.F. Red Arrows thrill crowds at airshows. Planes fly in close formation, changing position with split-second timing to perform different maneuvers.

The American X-15 was launched in mid-air from beneath a B-52 bomber. The pilot ignited the rocket engine, and the X-15 soared away into the stratosphere. It flew as high as 67.08 miles touching the fringes of outer space.

How does a helicopter hover?

DANGER

A helicopter is an aircraft with no wings or propellers. Instead it has a main rotor with long, slender blades. The rotor is turned by the helicopter's engine. As the rotor spins, the blades cut into the air. The air flowing over and under the blades produces an upward force, or "lift," just like an airplane's wing. The pilot can alter the angle of the blades to increase or decrease the amount of lift. Another smaller rotor at the back helps the helicopter to turn and holds it steady. A helicopter can generate enough lift to stay airborne without moving forward. So a helicopter can hover, or remain in the same spot. Helicopters carry out many dangerous missions, rescuing people from water and mountains.

More about air transport

Where was the first manned balloon flight?

The first balloon carrying human passengers took off from Paris on November 21, 1783. The balloon was a hot-air balloon made by the Montgolfier brothers. Josef-Michel and Jacques-Etienne Montgolfier based their idea of balloon flight on the fact that smoke from a fire always rises. After experimenting by lighting fires underneath balloons of cloth and paper, they offered to take passengers on board the real thing. The passengers were Jean Francois Pilatre de Rozier and the Marquis d'Arlandes, and their historic flight lasted twenty-three minutes.

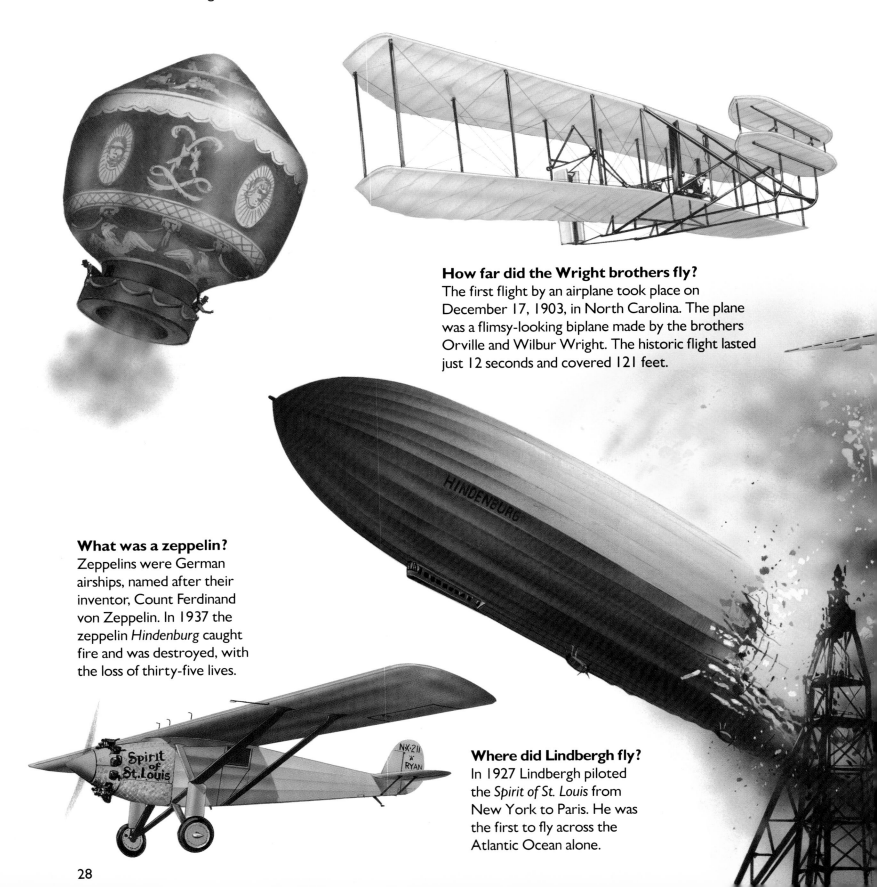

How far did the Wright brothers fly?

The first flight by an airplane took place on December 17, 1903, in North Carolina. The plane was a flimsy-looking biplane made by the brothers Orville and Wilbur Wright. The historic flight lasted just 12 seconds and covered 121 feet.

What was a zeppelin?

Zeppelins were German airships, named after their inventor, Count Ferdinand von Zeppelin. In 1937 the zeppelin *Hindenburg* caught fire and was destroyed, with the loss of thirty-five lives.

Where did Lindbergh fly?

In 1927 Lindbergh piloted the *Spirit of St. Louis* from New York to Paris. He was the first to fly across the Atlantic Ocean alone.

28

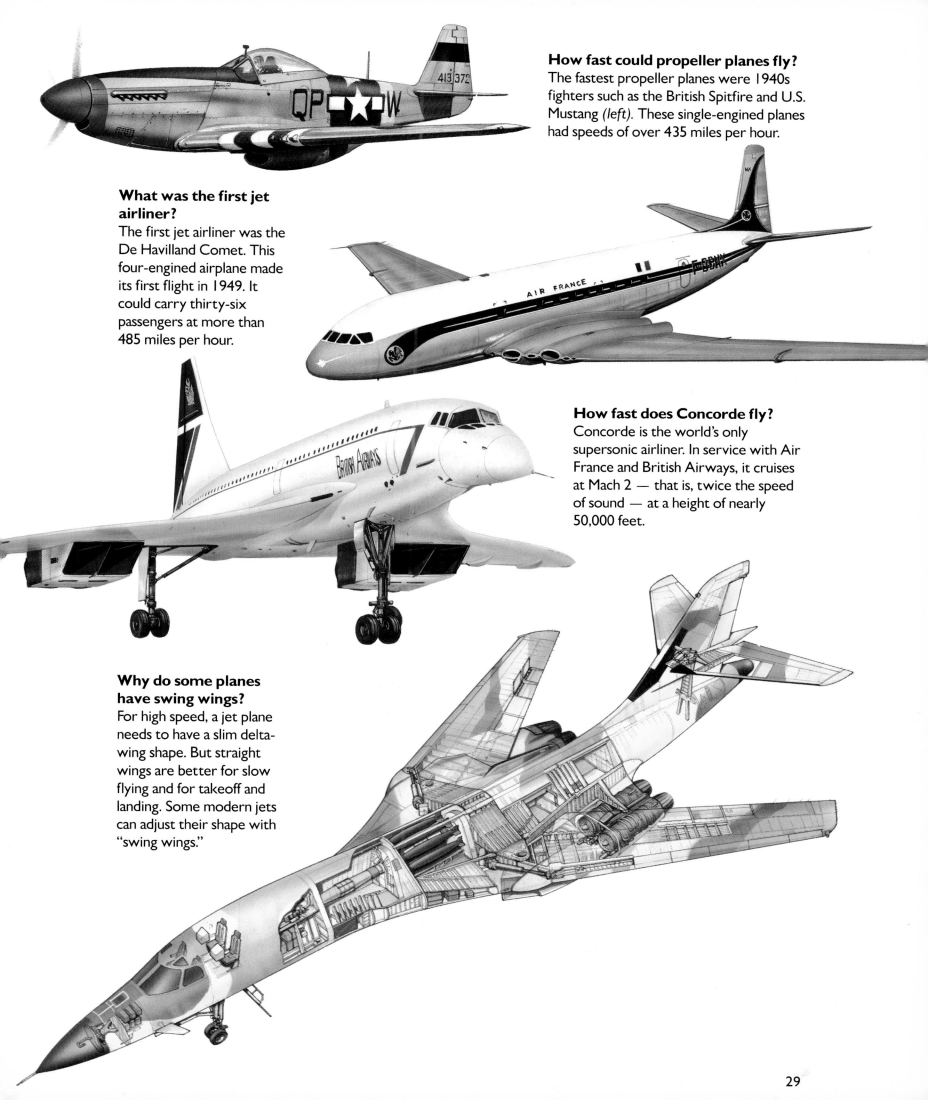

How fast could propeller planes fly?
The fastest propeller planes were 1940s fighters such as the British Spitfire and U.S. Mustang (left). These single-engined planes had speeds of over 435 miles per hour.

What was the first jet airliner?
The first jet airliner was the De Havilland Comet. This four-engined airplane made its first flight in 1949. It could carry thirty-six passengers at more than 485 miles per hour.

How fast does Concorde fly?
Concorde is the world's only supersonic airliner. In service with Air France and British Airways, it cruises at Mach 2 — that is, twice the speed of sound — at a height of nearly 50,000 feet.

Why do some planes have swing wings?
For high speed, a jet plane needs to have a slim delta-wing shape. But straight wings are better for slow flying and for takeoff and landing. Some modern jets can adjust their shape with "swing wings."

Why do most airliners have jet engines?

Four powerful turbofan jet engines push a Boeing 747 airliner, weighing more than 400 tons, into the sky. Jet engines give this giant of the air a speed of more than 600 miles per hour. That is faster than a fighter plane of World War II. In a jet engine, fuel and oxygen are burned to make a jet of very hot gas. The hot gas shoots out backward sending the plane forward at great speed. A turbofan engine has a fan that sucks air into the engine for extra power. The 747, the world's biggest jet airliner, first flew in 1969.

More about jets

The first jet plane was the German Heinkel He-178 (*above*), which first flew on August 27, 1939. Its jet engine was built by Pabst von Ohain. In Britain, the inventor Frank Whittle tested jet engines in the early 1930s. The first Whittle jet plane was the Gloster E28/39 of 1941.

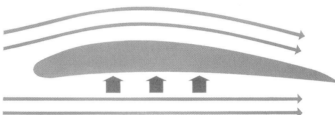

A plane flies because its wings provide an upward force known as "lift." The wing is curved on top and flat underneath. This causes air to flow faster over the wing than beneath it. There is reduced air pressure above the wing, which creates a suction effect above the wing. Air pressure on the flat bottom of the wing provides a lifting force.

A jet airliner needs a long runway for takeoff and landing. But a VTOL (vertical takeoff and landing) plane like the British Harrier can "jump" into the air, and does not need a runway. The Harrier's turbofan engine has swivel nozzles that direct the jet thrust at different angles. With the nozzles pointing downward, the plane takes off vertically.

How far can a plane fly nonstop?

With two people, Dick Rutan and Jeana Yeager, squeezed inside, the ultralightweight plane *Voyager* flew round the world nonstop in 1986. The flight of 26,661 miles took nine days. The twin-propeller *Voyager* was designed to fly slowly for very long distances. It had very long, narrow wings (like a glider) and a twin-boom body. Inside were seventeen fuel tanks filled with 1,900 gallons of fuel. Just 16 gallons of fuel were left when the plane landed in California after its record-breaking journey. It had flown around the world at an average speed of 115 miles per hour.

More about air records

The first nonstop flight across the Atlantic Ocean was on June 14 and 15, 1919. John Alcock and Arthur Whitten Brown of Britain flew a converted Vicker Vimy bomber from Newfoundland to Ireland.

In 1924 two U.S. Army Douglas seaplanes made the first flight around the world. Four planes set out. One crashed on a mountain and another sank at sea. The two planes that survived took 175 days (with stops) to complete the flight, a 26,345 - mile trip.

In 1979 the *Gossamer Albatross* became the first human-powered airplane to fly the English Channel. The pilot Bryan Allen pedaled to drive the chain that turned the lightweight plane's propeller. The journey took eight hours and forty minutes.

Where do yachts race?

Yachts are sailboats that race around courses marked by buoys. Yachts range in size from small dinghies sailing offshore or on an inland lake to large ocean racers. One of the most famous yacht races is the America's Cup. It began in 1851 as a race round the Isle of Wight, off southern England.

The winning yacht was a schooner named *America*, and the cup it won became known as The America's Cup. American yachts won the race twenty-four times in 132 years until 1983, when the Australian yacht *Australia II* defeated the American yacht *Liberty*.

LIBERTY
USA

Clippers were the fastest and most graceful of all big sailing ships. First built in the 1830s, clippers carried cargoes of tea from India and China, and wool from Australia. Clippers crossed the Atlantic in twelve days, and sailed from Australia to England in sixty days.

A catamaran is a twin-hulled boat. The idea comes from the outrigger canoe of the Pacific islands; the outrigger made the slender canoe more stable at sea. A catamaran can travel extremely fast because it has very little bottom to drag against the surface of the water.

Most ships today have steam turbines or diesel engines, burning oil. One day the world's oil supplies will run out, and ships may then rely more on wind power again. Some experimental sailing cargo ships are already at sea. They have high-technology sails, controlled by computers, to back up their engines.

More about transport at sea

What were the first ships like?
The first ships were built in Egypt about 4000 B.C. They were made of reeds, because there were few trees to provide timber, and were propelled by paddles as shown below. The first ships were used mainly on rivers. About 3000 B.C., Egyptian seamen sailed across the rougher waters of the Mediterranean in larger wooden ships with a mast carrying a single sail. The Phoenicians and the Greeks also built ships to cross the Mediterranean. In about 300 B.C. they built large ships with two sails for carrying cargo.

What was a galleon?
The galleon *(bottom left)* was the most important European sailing ship from the 1500s to the 1700s.

What were Viking longships?
From 800 A.D., Viking sea rovers from Scandinavia sailed the seas in wooden longships. These were narrow wooden vessels with room for about sixty rowers.

Where was the first steamship service?
The first regular steamship service did not begin until 1807. The *North River Steamboat of Clermont* steamed up and down the Hudson River.

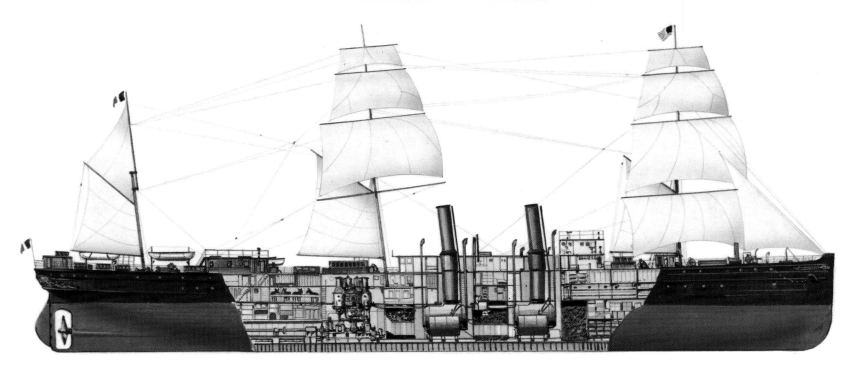

How early were screw propellers?

Screw propellers became standard on oceangoing steamships from the 1840s. The steam packet of the 1860s *(above)* still carried sails in case of engine breakdown.

Why did the *Titanic* sink?

In 1912 the *Titanic* hit an iceberg at night. Five compartments were holed, the engines broke free, and the ship sank in under two and a half hours. More than 1,500 people were drowned.

What was the first nuclear-powered ship?

Nuclear power was first tried at sea in the 1950s, mostly in submarines but also in surface ships. The Soviet icebreaker *Lenin* of 1957 was the world's first nuclear-powered ship.

How big are ocean liners?

The largest liner afloat is the *Norway* (formerly *France*) shown above, which is 1,033 feet long and has a gross tonnage of 70,202 tons. It was launched in 1961, and recommissioned with its new name in 1975. The heaviest liner ever was the *Queen Elizabeth* (1940-1968), at over 85,000 tons.

How do submarines dive?

A submarine can dive as deep as 2,600 feet into the ocean. A diving submarine increases its density by flooding ballast tanks with water. This makes the submarine sink. To surface, the tanks are "blown" by filling them with compressed air. The air pushes the water out through the valves in the hull. Now less dense than the water around it, the submarine rises.

More about submarines

Submarines underwater can take in air through breathing tubes called snorkels. The periscope is an arrangement of mirrors inside a tube which can be raised about fifty feet. This means the captain of a submerged submarine can spot ships on the surface without his own craft being spotted.

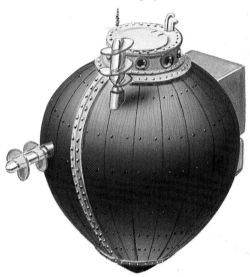

David Bushnell's *Turtle* was the first submarine to attack a warship. In 1776 the tiny one-man craft tried to blow up a British ship during the American Revolution. It was propelled by a hand cranked screw. The attack failed, but the *Turtle* survived.

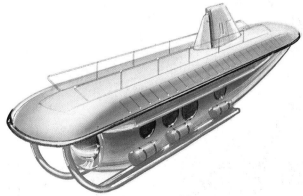

A submersible is a submarine used for industrial and scientific work. Small submersibles work on undersea oil pipelines. They carry powerful searchlights and television cameras.

What is the Space Shuttle?

The Space Shuttle is a reusable spacecraft. The main part of the Shuttle is the winged orbiter. Once in orbit, it can launch satellites or other space equipment such as telescopes. Astronauts leave the Shuttle to work in space, using the MMU, or manned maneuvering unit. This "flying seat" has small jet thrusters that propel the MMU through space. The Shuttle returns to earth after each mission and lands like an airplane on an airstrip.

More about the Shuttle

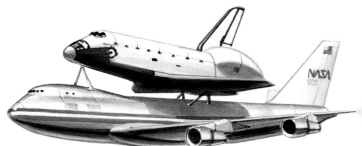

The American Shuttle was tested in the earth's atmosphere before it ever went into space. It was carried piggyback on top of a specially modified Boeing 747 airplane. After release high above ground, the Shuttle glided back to earth. These tests taught pilots how to land the spacecraft.

The Soviet Union's Shuttle is called *Buran,* or *Snowstorm.* It is the same shape as the American Shuttle, but unlike the American craft, *Buran* uses engines when coming in to land.

The most dangerous part of a Shuttle flight is reentry into the earth's atmosphere. The spacecraft is moving very fast. As it hits the air in the upper atmosphere, friction makes the spacecraft red-hot, like a fireball plunging earthward. The Shuttle is coated with a heat shield of tiles. The tiles slowly char, absorbing the heat and protecting the crew inside.

More about transport in space

What was the first real space rocket?
The Chinese used rockets as long ago as the 1200s. But the first rocket big enough to be fired into space was the German V-2. The V-2 was the first long-range rocket-powered missile. It stood forty-six feet high. On October 3, 1942 the V-2 was successfully launched when it reached an altitude of 53 miles. After World War II, the Americans and Russians used captured V-2s to begin their space programs. One of the V-2's designers was Wernher von Braun, who built the giant Saturn 5 rocket used to send American astronauts to the moon.

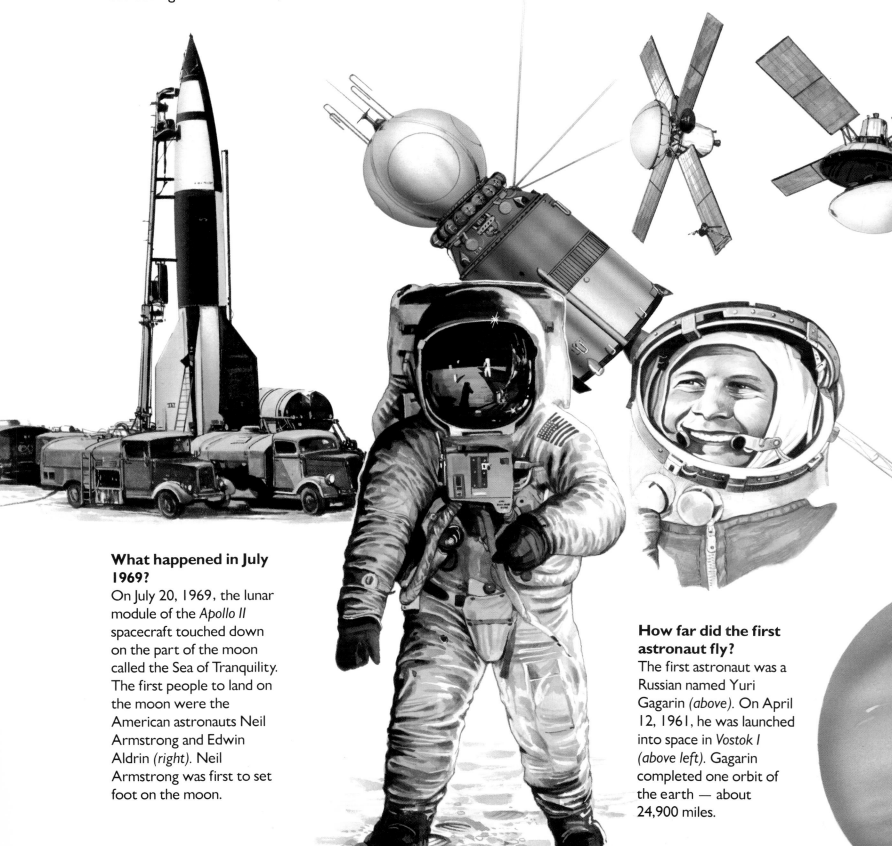

What happened in July 1969?
On July 20, 1969, the lunar module of the *Apollo II* spacecraft touched down on the part of the moon called the Sea of Tranquility. The first people to land on the moon were the American astronauts Neil Armstrong and Edwin Aldrin *(right)*. Neil Armstrong was first to set foot on the moon.

How far did the first astronaut fly?
The first astronaut was a Russian named Yuri Gagarin *(above)*. On April 12, 1961, he was launched into space in *Vostok I (above left)*. Gagarin completed one orbit of the earth — about 24,900 miles.

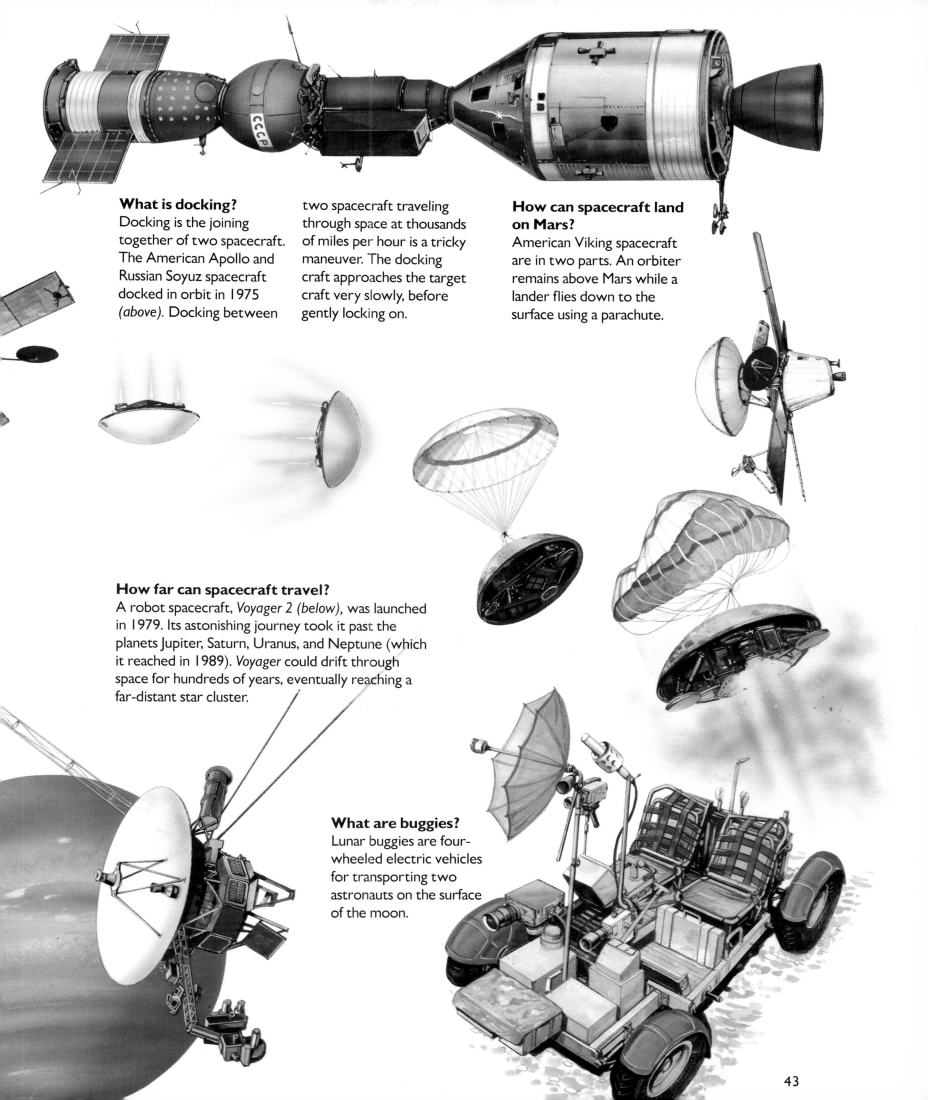

What is docking?

Docking is the joining together of two spacecraft. The American Apollo and Russian Soyuz spacecraft docked in orbit in 1975 (above). Docking between two spacecraft traveling through space at thousands of miles per hour is a tricky maneuver. The docking craft approaches the target craft very slowly, before gently locking on.

How can spacecraft land on Mars?

American Viking spacecraft are in two parts. An orbiter remains above Mars while a lander flies down to the surface using a parachute.

How far can spacecraft travel?

A robot spacecraft, Voyager 2 (below), was launched in 1979. Its astonishing journey took it past the planets Jupiter, Saturn, Uranus, and Neptune (which it reached in 1989). Voyager could drift through space for hundreds of years, eventually reaching a far-distant star cluster.

What are buggies?

Lunar buggies are four-wheeled electric vehicles for transporting two astronauts on the surface of the moon.

43

How does the *Ariane* rocket work?

The European *Ariane* rocket is used to launch satellites into orbit. Its main launch site is in French Guiana in South America. The *Ariane* stands about 164 feet high. It is made up of stages or steps. The first stage contains the main engines, which lift the heavy rocket off the launchpad. When its fuel is used up, the first stage falls away and the second stage engine fires. Finally, the third-stage motor fires to take the rocket into orbit high above the earth. The *Ariane* is known as an ELV, or expendable launch vehicle, because each rocket can be used once only. ELVs are less complicated and cheaper than Shuttles.

More about the launch of *Ariane*

The *Ariane* rocket has solid-fuel booster rockets to give extra power on takeoff. Lift-off looks quite slow, for the first-stage engine has to lift the massive weight of the rocket. The rocket gains speed steadily because as it uses up fuel it becomes lighter.

After about two minutes, the boosters and the first-stage engine burn out. The first stage falls away, and the smaller second-stage engine fires.

When the second stage is released, the third-stage engine sends the payload into orbit. A satellite released 340 miles above the earth makes one orbit every one and a half hours. A satellite orbiting at over 22,300 miles takes twenty-four hours to circle the earth. By keeping up with the speed of the earth's rotation, it can stay above one point on the earth's surface and relay telephone signals.

INDEX

AN ILEX BOOK
Created and produced by Ilex Publishers Limited
29-31 George Street, Oxford, OX1 2AJ

Main illustrations by Sebastian Quigley/Linden Artists Ltd
Other illustrations by Sebastian Quigley, Tony Bryan and Hardlines